For my family

DingDong Batty

Ding Dong Batty

Gemma Beedham

Ding Dong Batty was a very scatty bat

who loved to fly around in his big bright hat.

He'd fly by day but mostly at night,

making noises on his flight.

As Batty was a Ding Dong bat,

The noise he made was exactly that.

He'd ding dong here, he'd ding dong there,

he'd ding dong almost everywhere.

He'd Ding Dong high.

He'd Ding Dong low.

He'd Ding Dong fast.

He'd Ding Dong slow

He'd Ding Dong quiet.

Ding Dong

He'd Ding Dong loud

He'd Ding Dong bold.

He'd Ding Dong proud

All the bats from miles around

could hear his crazy ding dong sound

and thought of it as bad and wrong

as it was not their usual one.

Batty did not seem to care

and kept ding donging everywhere.

When they heard him on his way

they would look up in the air and say,

"Oh no, it is that ding dong bat,

the one who wears the big bright hat.

Don't come here, go away,

we don't want you, not today."

A few days later, late at night

whilst ding donging on his flight,

he heard a really awful sound,

a kind of rumbling from the ground.

Knowing something was quite wrong

he went to see what had gone on.

It seemed that there had been a quake,

which caused the earth to move and shake.

Where there were once caves before

was now just rubble on the floor.

All the bats trapped underground

heard Batty's crazy ding dong sound.

They knew that they would be ok

as help would soon be on it's way.

Ding Dong Batty strong and brave,

made his way into the cave.

Moving rubble left and right,

helping all the bats in sight.

Batty made his ding dong sound

and led the bats from underground.

When they were all safe and free,

they flew around with joy and glee.

They shouted "hip hip hooray,"

Ding Dong Batty saved the day.

Now when they hear him on his way

they look up in the sky and say,

"Oh, it's Ding Dong Batty, the most amazing bat,

the one who wears the big bright hat."

"Please come here," we want to say,

"Come and play with us today."

Batty is now a famous bat,

and still wears his big bright hat.

He can hear bats from miles around

make his crazy ding dong sound.